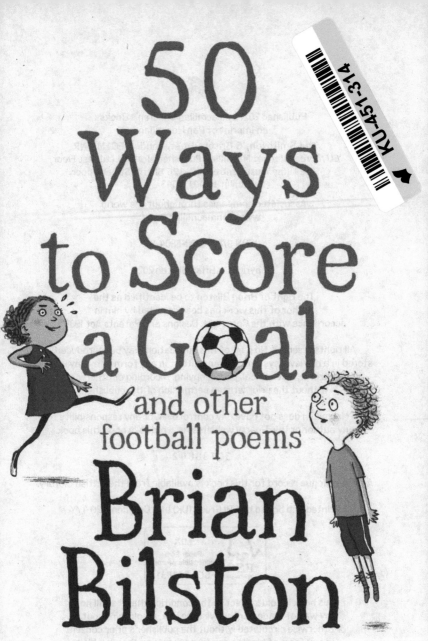

50
Ways
to Score
a Goal
and other
football poems

Brian
Bilston

MACMILLAN CHILDREN'S BOOKS

Published 2021 by Macmillan Children's Books
an imprint of Pan Macmillan

The Smithson, 6 Briset Street, London EC1M 5NR
EU representative: Macmillan Publishers Ireland Ltd, 1st Floor,
The Liffey Trust Centre, 117–126 Sheriff Street Upper,
Dublin 1, D01 YC43

Associated companies throughout the world
www.panmacmillan.com

ISBN 978-1-5290-5804-8

3 5 7 9 8 6 4 2

A CIP catalogue record for this book is available from the British Library.

Printed and bound by CPI Group (UK) Ltd, Croydon CR0 4YY

MIX
Paper from
responsible sources
FSC® C116313

Contents

First Half

Half-Time

Second Half

First Half ⚽

Kick-Off

And here he comes,
emerging through the tunnel
to the roar of the crowd,
striding out to the centre circle,
where he sits down at his desk.

He does a few keepy-ups with his pen
to keep the nerves at bay,
and then come the handshakes –
with the cat, the reader –
as the coin is flipped high,

twisting and turning in the air,
spinning gold. An exchange of nods,
the blow of a whistle,
he turns the page over
and he's off!

Football Is . . .

Football is . . .
Football is a wiggle of the hips
Football is a whistle to the lips
Football is late-night fish and chips
Football is

Football is an unwritten poem
Football is trousers in need of sewing
Football is days off when it's snowing
Football is

Football is a scrambled goal line clearance
Football is a school bell disappearance
Football is a blind adherence
Football is

Football is a language that's universal
Football is a perfect centre circle
Football's the real thing not a rehearsal
Football is

Football is a door without need of a key
Football is one thing for you, another for me
Football is whatever you want it to be
Football is . . .

Pick Me!

Pick your brain
Pick your nose
Pick your pocket
Pick a rose
Pick an apple
(from a tree)
Pick a winner
PICK ME!

AMY...　　　　　　*DAN...*
VEROUSHKA...　　*STAN...*
WILLIAM...　　　　*CARRIE...*
MUHAMMED...　　*HARRY...*

Pick your battles
Pick a bone
Pick up speed
Pick up the phone
Pick a scab
(from your knee)
Pick your moment
PICK ME!

IBRAHIM...
CHLOE...
ALFIE...
ZOE...
GREGORY...
NADIM...
LISA...
SELENE...

Pick a fight
Pick up sticks
Pickled herring
Pick and mix
Pick a lock
(set me free)
Pick of the bunch
PICK ME!

LOGAN...
DANIEL...
KELLY...
SAMUEL...
SAMANTHA...
NICK...

Two left...
I'll have VIC...

OK, then, BRIAN.

YIPPEE!
I GOT PICKED!!!

7

Trevor

One of the best things
about having an imaginary friend
is always having someone
to play football with.

Trevor never lets me down.
He's always happy to go in goal
when I want to practise penalties.
Whenever I give the ball to him, he'll pass it back
and not laugh, like the others,
if I don't manage to control it.

The only annoying thing about Trevor
is that when he gets called in
for his imaginary tea,
he takes his imaginary ball with him.

An Educated Left Foot

Have you heard?
He's got an educated left foot.

It's got twenty-seven GCSEs,
ten A-levels
and three degrees.

It's Professor
of Footballology,
at the University of Parks.

No matter what exam it takes,
it always passes
with top marks.

His right foot,
on the other hand
(a strange place for one, I have to say),

couldn't pass
the time of day.

Formations

Right, team, let's talk formation.
I'm a genius, me.
It's just simple mathematics.
We'll play 4-4-3.

What's that? Too many players?
I've counted one more?
Sorry, a slip of the tongue.
I meant 5-2-4.

That's *still* wrong, you say?
Oh, I see what I've done!
I must have counted the goalie –
we'll go 3-5-1.

I'm a master tactician...
oh, what now? I've too *few*?
In that case, how about we play
...3–4–2?
Or 5–1–3?
4–2–5?
6–3–4?
5–2–3–1?

Hang on, where are you all going?
What do you mean, you'll see me later?
I command you to stay! Please come back!
Anyone got a calculator?

The Laws of the Game (Playground edition)

1. The field of play must be a wholly natural playing surface; it should be rectangular and marked with continuous lines
    OR
    it can be a peculiarly shaped strip of unforgiving tarmac, bordered on one side by the new science block, and the bicycle racks on the other.

2. The penalty spot should be situated 10.97m (12yds) from the midpoint between the goalposts
    OR
    about 6 paces from the goal line (4½ paces if you're Kieran Thomas because he's got really long legs and his strides are MASSIVE).

3. A goal consists of two vertical posts joined by a horizontal crossbar. The distance between the inside of the posts is 7.32m (8yds) and the distance from the crossbar to the ground is 2.44m (8ft)
    OR

*just bung any bags or jumpers down in two
unruly piles at each end, then adjust until piles
are roughly equidistant* and the arguing stops.*

**Ensure at all times that someone keeps an
eye on Elaine Jenkins because she's always
shortening the width of her goal when no one's
looking.*

4. The ball must be spherical, be made of a suitable
   material, be of a circumference between 68cm
   and 70cm, weigh between 410g and 450g, and be
   of a pressure of 0.6 – 1.1 atmosphere at sea level
   OR
   *belong to Craig Simmons, although he said he
   might not bring it in today after what happened
   yesterday lunchtime.*

5. A match is played between two teams, each with
   a maximum of eleven players, one of whom must
   be the goalkeeper
   OR
   maybe just wait and see how many turn up,

although more than 16-a-side does make the game rather cramped.

When picking teams, remember that Claire Scott is worth at least two players, and that she and Karim Shah are not allowed to play on the same team because that just isn't fair.

6. Each match is controlled by a referee who has full authority to enforce the Laws of the Game in connection with the match
    OR
    in the event of no referee being available, decisions should be argued about for several minutes until either
    a) a resolution is reached,
    b) a fight breaks out,
    c) or Craig Simmons takes his ball away again.

7. A match lasts for two equal halves of 45 minutes.
    OR
    as is more likely, the school bell rings, and the players have to go inside for stupid French or Geography.

8. The team that wins the toss of a coin decides which goal to attack in the first half or to take the kick-off
OR
alternatively, the decision as to which team should take the kick-off may simply depend on whose ball is being used (please refer to regulation 4, final paragraph).

9. A goal is scored when the whole of the ball passes over the goal line, between the posts and under the crossbar, provided that no offence has been committed by the team scoring the goal
OR
in the event of no crossbar being available, the ball must not have exceeded the height of the goalkeeper by more than the length of a standard 30cm shatterproof ruler.
Remember, in the event of goal / post disputes, it is possible to award ½ a goal.

10. A player is in an offside position if any part of the head, body or feet is nearer to the opponents' goal line than both the ball and

the second-last opponent
OR
you may deem it impractical to enforce the offside rule. Blatant goal hanging is to be frowned upon, however, and any player found guilty of such may find themselves the subject of disapproving looks from their classmates for the rest of the day.

11. The team scoring the greater number of goals is the winner. If both teams score no goals or an equal number of goals the match is drawn
OR
given both the high frequency of goals scored, and the number of disputed goal decisions, it may be unclear as to what the final result is. In such circumstances, it is customary for one last round of arguments before afternoon lessons begin, and then for the match to be replayed the following lunchtime, and all future lunchtimes thereafter.

WONDERKID!

Introducing . . . FOOTBALL'S latest WONDERKID!
She's worth EIGHTY-SEVEN MILLION QUID
Won the BALLON D'OR
When she was FOUR
There's RUMOURS she's off to REAL MADRID

Since from OBSCURITY she was PLUCKED
She's already LIFTED the FA CUP
By the age of SIX
She knew all the TRICKS
She's WORLD RECORD HOLDER for KEEPY-UPS

She's the YOUNGEST EVER ENGLAND RECRUIT
She's the HOLDER of the GOLDEN BOOT
An all-time GREAT
And she's only EIGHT
She can't get past GRADE 3 on the FLUTE

WONDERKID TO MISS WORLD CUP FINAL SHOCK!!!
SPECULATION RIFE: HAS SHE BEEN DROPPED?
Her mum sets things straight:
'It kicks off too late
And she NEEDS to be IN BED by NINE O'CLOCK'

The Intergalactic Super Cup Final

I like the FA Cup, the Premier and Champions Leagues
and the World Cup, I suppose, has a certain prestige,
but they're not much to sing about –
    mere kickabout trifles –
compared with the Intergalactic Super Cup Final.

The tournament takes place every four light years
    or so,
with the brightest stars from each galaxy on show.
The games are beamed around space (complete
    with subtitles):
billions watch the Intergalactic Super Cup Final.

This year the final is being played on Outer Zygon 9.
A more distant planet you'd be hard pressed to find.
It takes a space age by astrobus (and far longer to
    cycle)
to get to the Intergalactic Super Cup Final.

And here comes Xubulia in their green and white
    stripes
(they don't wear a kit, they just have green and
    white stripes).
They're playing Tendrillus 12 – their keen local rivals –
to contest the Intergalactic Super Cup Final.

What happened to Earth? They played Quatermass
    Edge
and got knocked out in the first round over three legs
(Earthlings only have two – even Cristiano and Lionel.
Not enough for the Intergalactic Super Cup Final).

The final itself was an entertaining affair:
Tendrillus 12 playing with a tentacled flair,
Telepathic Xubulia more measured and mindful,
in an end-to-end Intergalactic Super Cup Final.

With the tension rising, two of the players saw red
(the ref must have had eyes in the back of his head).
Into the last minute, the score tied at five-all . . .
Who will win the Intergalactic Super Cup Final?

The winner, in added time, was the pick of the bunch.
A breathless counter-attack with a quick sucker punch,
The Tendrillus striker getting that last touch so vital
to win the Intergalactic Super Cup Final.

A match out of this world. The fans over the moon.
And then, across the galaxies, the stars sang a tune
of cosmic togetherness; a heavenly recital
to honour the Intergalactic Super Cup Final.

Fifty Ways to Score a Goal

tap in, toe poke, thunderbolt,
backheel, nutmeg, stinger,
glancing header, mis-hit cross,
rebound, blaster, zinger

goalkeeping blunder, penalty,
curler, sidefoot, prod,
scissors, volley (full and half)
scorcher, Hand of God

rocket, drill, fire, lash it in,
bundle, drive, stab, chip,
screamer, belter, slam, caress,
bum, shin, chin, knee, hip

diving header, outrageous lob,
deflection, quick free-kick,
finesse, stroke, steer, walk it in,
dink, punt, slot and flick

Fifty Slow Motion Replays

taaap innn, tooooooe pokke, thuuuunderbolt,
baaackheeeeel, nuttttmeggg, stiiiingerrr,
glaaaancing headddder, missssss-hittttt
    crosssss,
reeeeeeebound, blaaaaster, ziiiiinger

goalkeeeeeeping blunderrrrrr, pennnnnalty,
currrrrler, sidefooooooooot, prodddddd,
scisssssssors, vollllllley (fulllll and halfffff)
scorrrrrrcher, Hannnd of Goddd

rockkkkket, drrrrrillll, fiiiiire, lashhhhh it in,
bunnnndle, driiiive, stabbbbb, chipppp,
screeeeeeamer, bellllller, slammmmm,
    caressssss,
bummmmm, shinnnnn, chinnnn, kneeeeeeee,
    hippppp

diiiiving headddder, outraaaaaageous lobb,
deeeeflection, quiiiick freeeee-kickkkk,
finesssssse, strrrrroke, steeeeeeer, wallllk it in,
dinnnk, punnnnt, slottttt and flickkkk

The Language of Football

There's a new boy in my class.
He came here from far away.
He doesn't speak any English.
Can't make out a word I say.

But at lunchtime, we play football
and it's like we are old friends.
We share a common language
with no need of books or pens.

We do our talking with our feet;
we communicate each pass.
He leaves the bombed-out streets behind
and forgets the sudden blasts

for a little while. Here, *shots fired*
doesn't mean the same at all;
attacks are just a chance to score;
a *volley* is an un-bounced ball.

I look at him. We share a smile.
The game swings from end to end.
I lose the ball. He wins it back
and then starts to build again.

Keepie-Uppies

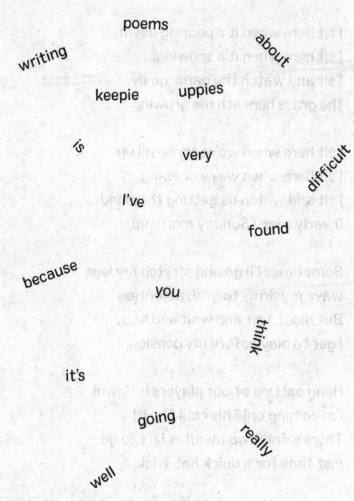

poems

writing

about

keepie   uppies

is

very

difficult

I've

found

because

you

think

it's

going

really

well

but then it ends up on the ground

25

On the Bench

I sit here when it's pouring down.
I sit here when it's snowing.
I sit and watch the game go by,
the grass beneath me growing.

I sit here when we're three-nil up.
I sit here when we're drawing.
I sit and watch us getting thrashed
(nearly every Sunday morning).

Sometimes I'll go and stretch my legs,
wave my arms to grab attention.
But most, I sit and wait and hope
I get to play before my pension.

Hang on! One of our players is down!
I'm coming on! This could be it!
There's only two minutes left to go –
just time for a quick hat-trick.

The Thing About Wingers

the
thing
about
wing-
ers
is
that
they
like
to
stay
out
wide
but
every
now
and
then
(you
won't
guess
when)
they will
suddenly
cut inside

A Suggestion

Mum and Dad were laughing;
it seemed as good a moment as any
to suggest that we all move
to the Faroe Islands.

I could sense some bemusement on their part –
and beneath that, reluctance –
so I fired up PowerPoint
and set about things.

Did you know, I said,
pointing to a picture of a wind farm,
that the Faroe Islands is
one of the world's leading users
of renewable energy?

They had no idea. One-nil to me!

Emboldened, I went on.
The average life expectancy in the Faroe Islands,
I told them, is 82.24 years.
Compare that to the mere 80.96 years
we get here in the UK, I said.

They nodded encouragingly.
Two-nil, surely.

The next slide contained a photo of a Faroese bus.
Did you know, I said –
moving in for the clincher –
that bus travel in the capital, Tórshavn,
is completely free?

They looked impressed. Three-nil.
There could be no backing out now.
If there are any questions from the audience, I said,
I will be happy to answer them.

Dad piped up. I've heard, he said,
there are more sheep on the Faroe Islands
than there are people.
I nodded. 20,000 more, I told him.
Dad must have been doing his own research:
this was even better than I'd thought!

Mmm, I see, he said.
And I suppose you think, he continued,
that if we were to move to the Faroe Islands
this might be your best chance
to play international football when you're older.

No, I said. Absolutely not! Ha, ha!
Hadn't crossed my mind once, I said convincingly.
Not one single time! Never! Hah!
No, no, no, no, not at all.

They were both eyeing me suspiciously.
It was time to switch to Plan B.
I opened up a new presentation.
San Marino, I informed them,
claims to be the world's oldest republic . . .

O.G.

Opening game.
Overgrown grass.
Overhit goof.
Onlookers gasp.

Oblivious goalie.
Ostentatiously garbed.
Oncoming gloom.
Off goal-line. Off guard.

Optimistic gyrations.
Outwitted gloves.
Ominous glare.
Open-mouthed gulp.

Over goal-line.
Opposition glee.
OWN GOAL! Oh, golly.
Oh, goodness. Oh, gee.

Total Football

People say I'm obsessed with football
so I thought I would penalty a quick rhyme
to prove instead, there's more in my header
and I don't think about it all the time added on.

I admit I liked it when I was four-four-two
but that was a long time Aguero, for sure.
I've Cruyff-turned over a Neuer leaf, you see,
and I don't think about it Neymar.

Centre-back then, I was total football.
It took me overhead kick, I confess.
It blew through my life like a Harry Kane.
I was miseraBale. A complete Messi.

Mo Salah time now I don't think about it.
I'm a changed Man United, you see.
I've cleared my mind. I've cleared my lines.
A new life Beckhams for me.

Football Haikus: Starting XI

I

Goalkeeper standing
between two tall kangaroos.
Jumpers for goalposts.

II

We've signed a legend.
He is half-human, half-horse.
Plays centaur-forward.

III

Haiku Town line up:
5-7-5 formation.
Too many players.

IV

Cinderella dropped.
She ran away from the ball.
Pumpkin for a coach.

V

Please spare a thought for
the assistant referee:
he's started to flag.

VI

Footballer dancing
at a grand party for ghosts.
Dead ball specialist.

VII

Vampire goalie
gets it in the neck from crowd.
Can't handle crosses.

VIII

A chicken gets booked
and asks the referee why:
persistent fowl play.

IX
Corner is taken.
Match gets abandoned due to
a lopsided pitch.

X
Referee wanted.
Satisfaction guaranteed.
Whistle while you work.

XI
It's a penalty!
She puts the ball on the spot,
runs up, strikes it and

Matchday

Matchday tastes different to other days.
It tastes of mint humbugs and half-time soup.
It can be as bitter as Grandad's coffee,
as salty as tears, or sour like vinegar on bus stop chips,
but sometimes it's sweet as icing on a cake,
or a perfectly struck volley.

Matchday sounds different to other days.
It's sirens and roars and rude words and shouts
and songs and whistles and silence,
but not just any old silence, the kind of silence
that exists between the striking of the ball
and the rippling of the net.

Matchday smells different to other days.
It smells of intercity trains and local buses,
armpits and freshly printed programmes,
onions frying in roadside vans. And on the wind,
you might catch the scent of anticipation
and hope, always hope.

Matchday feels different to other days.
It can be as soft as freshly laid turf.
It can be hard like a plastic seat
or an uncompromising centre-half.
It can slip through your fingers like a greasy ball.
It can warm you like a scarf.

Matchday looks different to other days.
It wears colours organized by stripes or hoops.
It is blurs and sharpened edges,
straight lines, curves, and shifting shapes.
It is gloom and sunshine and floodlit brilliance.
You take these pictures home with you.

Matchday is different to other days.

A Cautionary Tale

My dad's a referee.
It can make life very hard.
He can barely last five minutes
without reaching for a card.

He dishes them out at dinner.
He serves them up with tea.
He writes my name down in his book.
He does this regularly.

He finds a way to caution me
no matter the situation.
I dived on to the sofa once:
got a card for simulation.

He's a stickler for the rules.
He's unbending, mean and stringent.
I'd like to let my hair grow long
but he'd book me for infringement.

I didn't eat my cabbage salad
and he waved a card at me –
for denying an obvious
coleslawing opportunity.

I get yellow cards every day,
they're not easy to prevent.
And when I tell him it's not fair,
he books me for dissent.

At least he's never sent me off.
I must be grateful, I suppose.
And it seems to make him happy:
he whistles everywhere he goes.

Early Morning Goalkeeping Routine

Wake up. Yawn.
Stretch your arms ten times
(as high as they will go).
Get out of bed with a sideways roll.
Practise catching your pillow.

Remember it's Sunday.
Return to bed with a single leap.
Command your area at all times.
Dive under the covers.
Go back to sleep.

Two hours later, repeat:
being careful not to spill
your bedside glass of water
or you might spoil
your clean sheet.

A Shaggy Dog Story

my human love me lots
me his pride and joy
my tail go waggy wag
when he say good boy

my human brush my coat
he stroke and tickle snout
he give me special treat
we go big day out

me trot trot by his side
me make human proud
he take me to big park
big park very loud

lots of human here
they shouty noisy tall
me not see for legs
but then me see ... BALL!

oh how me love you ball
bestest ever friend
lovely lovely ball
on me you can depend

me jump over fence
me hear human call
me pretend me deaf
me go play with ball

oh how me love you ball
dribble rolly sniff
lovely lovely ball
rolly dribble lick

here come shouty man
dressed up all in black
he want to take my ball
me not give it back

many human chase
many human beg
me spin and turn and swerve
me run between their legs

42

last human up ahead
my ball he try to get
me too fast me run past
lovely ball in net

big park makes big roar
sing *gonna win the cup*
many human hug
one in suit comes up

says *sign your paw print here*
such wonderful technique
just the player we need
me come back next week

Lucky Bobble Hat

Now, please don't get me wrong,
I'm *not* superstitious
but I always wear my lucky bobble hat
to every match.

One time we scored this amazing goal.
Quick throw in. A few passes.
Moving through the gears.
Then, all of sudden, the old one-two.
Back of the net. Keeper no chance.
Bish, bash, bosh.

Just like a sharp knife slicing
through an over-ripe avocado, it was.
I don't really like avocado
but I'll save that story for another day.

And what did I 'just happen'
to have on my head at the time?
That's right. You guessed it.

Now, I'm *not* saying my bobble hat
was the reason we scored.
I'll let you draw your own conclusions.
But you can't deny I was wearing it
nor say the goal wasn't brilliant.

And that's why you'll always see me
wearing my lucky bobble hat on matchday.

Sometimes, I wonder
what might happen if I forgot it.
If word got out, I expect the players
wouldn't even bother
to emerge from the tunnel.

That's why I also make sure
I've got my lucky conker in my pocket, too.
You can never be too careful.
Not that I'm superstitious.

Honest Football Chants

I

We're the best team in the land,
Oh, we're the best team in the l—   *No, you're not!*

We're the next best team in the land,
Oh, we're the next best team in th— *Not even close.*

We're the best team in the town,
Oh, we're the best team in the t—   *Nope.*

We're the best team on the pitch,
Oh, we're the best team on the pi—   *You're losing
                                     eight-nil!*

We're a football team, yes we are.
Oh, we're a football team, yes we are.
We're a football team, yes we are.
Yes, we're a football team.   *Only just.
                                      But that will do.*

II

When you walk through a storm
Hold your brolly high
And please don't forget your cagoule

At the end of a storm
There's a golden sky
Or the clouds might not have gone at all

Walk on through the wind
Walk on through the rain
Though your feet be cold and wet

Walk on, walk on
Rain soaking your socks
And you'll never walk again

in such weather
without appropriate footwear.
I'd recommend a pair of wellies.

III

He's got the whole world in his hands.
He's got the whole wide world in his hands.
He's got the whole world in his hands.
Look at the size of his goalie gloves!

IV

I'm forever blowing bubbles,
Pretty bubbles in the air.
I just can't stop
Buying gum from the shop,
I chew it then blow
till it goes POP!

V

COME ON, YOU BLUES!

Unless, that is, we're playing away
then, of course, it's . . .
COME ON, YOU GREYS!

Assuming there's not a clash, that is,
in which case, we play in red
(although last season, I seem to recall
our shirts were pink instead).

But then, if it's a Tuesday
we wear hoops of white and green.
And for the European games,
either black or tangerine.

And now I come to think of it,
there may well be lots of others.
Perhaps it's safest just to sing:

COME ON, TEAM OF MANY COLOURS!

Transfer List

I'm on the transfer list.
It's pointless to resist.
I'm moving on,
I'll soon be gone,
I don't think I'll be missed.

The time has come, I know.
They need to let me go.
I take up space,
I'm out of place,
I'll leave in a half a mo.

It's Deadline Day today.
Suppose I'm on my way.
My face don't fit,
So on with it,
It's clear that I can't stay.

D-DAY MIDNIGHT TWIST!
I'm off the transfer list!
I'd packed my bag
but Mum and Dad
said where do you think you're going at this time
come and have a nice cup of hot chocolate

Fixtures

I'd love nothing more than to go outside
and spend time with Mother Nature.
But what can I do? It's out of my hands:
Nigeria are playing Croatia.

Eating on your own isn't much fun.
Some say there's nothing bleaker.
But this is the big one. I've waited all day.
Switzerland – Costa Rica.

Sorry to miss Gran's party today.
Please save me a piece of cake.
She'll understand, it's Morocco – Iran:
there's an awful lot at stake.

Yes, I know I've exams tomorrow.
I'll get revising as soon as I can.
Just ten minutes more (plus time added on)
of Colombia versus Japan.

League Table

1. Top of the table
2. Breathing down your neck
3. Challenging for the title
4 Not quite out of it yet
5. A solid bet for Europe
6. End of the chasing pack
7. Hoping for a final surge
8. Season still on track
9. Promise for the future
10. Comfortable security
11. Top of the bottom half
12. Drifting towards obscurity
13. Fading into nothingness
14. Won some, lost some, drew some
15. Pulling clear of danger
16. Current form is gruesome
17. Looking over shoulder
18. Bottom three since October
19. Praying for a miracle
20. Please let it all be over

A Football Squad of Collective Nouns

A flurry of yellow cards
A versatility of roles
A thwarting of woodwork
A blunder of own goals

A raft of substitutions
A net total of goalkeepers
A host of opportunities
A puddle of dribblers

A hatful of chances
A catalogue of errors
A dedication of fans
A flock of wingers

A matchbox of strikers
A crunch of tackles
An illumination of floodlights
A spray of passes

A trolley of volleys
A red mist of dismissals
A bag of chips
A heard of whistles

Half-Time ⚽

Right, time for a break from all the poems about football.

Here . . . have a half-time ~~orange~~ satsuma:

Half-Time ~~Orange~~ Satsuma

O how I love to consume a satsuma!
A satsuma a day leads to good humour.
I would wrestle a lion, a tiger or puma
for one sweet bite of a juicy satsuma.

O how I love to consume a satsuma!
I would risk the revenge of cruel Montezuma
or praise it in song, with the viola and tuba,
for one luscious segment of juicy satsuma.

O how I love to consume a satsuma!
I would travel the world – to Belgium or Cuba,
Pakistan, Chile, Guatemala, Bermuda,
for one single taste of a juicy satsuma.

O how I love to consume a satsuma!
Did I mention that before? It's true, not a rumour!
The fruit beloved of the poet and crooner
on account of it being far easier to rhyme
than the orange.

Second Half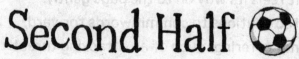

A Poem of Two Halves

This is a poem of two halves.
The opening lines are tentative and cagey.
It feels its way on to the page gently,
too cautious to commit words forward,
not offering much of an attacking threat.

Opportunities for a more interesting poem
are closed down quickly
as the first half draws tamely to a close.
It looks like the kind of poem,
that's got nil-nil written all over it.

—————————

The words are back out for the second half
but they're not really going anywhere
and there's a real danger this poem
might fizzle out completely . . .

but then FROM OUT OF NOWHERE one of the lines
goes on a long and mazy run right into
the heart
of the poem's defence,
the readers ROAR
and the whole poem EXPLODES into life!
A quick breakaway at the other end
results in a word hitting the P
O
S
T

The poem is opening up now – and about time!
Before we know it, there's even the odd rhyme
or two and then SUDDENLY

a word

finds itself in space,
sلəʌıʍs
and shoots,
past the outstretched
letters of the next line
AND IT'S A GOAL!

Then,

before the

poem   has had

a chance

to regroup,

in another **BOLD ATTACK**,
there's a second!*

For the rest of the poem, the wordplay
goes kcab and forwards, forwards and kcab.
Thereisbarelytimeforthereadertodrawbreath.

One word is ~~substituted~~ replaced by another
but it's all far too late now,
the writer signalling the end of the poem
with this full stop.

* One line protests too much and gets sent off, having to spend
the rest of the poem in a footnote.

64

A Ball Speaks Out

Well, officer, I was just sitting there,
minding my own business,
relishing my roundness
and thinking about the spherical nature of my
   existence,
when this fella runs up to me
and WHACK!

Yeah, that's right. In the park, it was.
Last Saturday afternoon.
About three o'clock, it must have been.
Anyway, then all these other fellas joined in
and they're running around
and kicking me all over the place!

They're shouting and screaming
and I'm pinging around like there's no tomorrow.
If it wasn't for the fact that I'm a ball,
I'd have the bruises to prove it.
I was feeling pretty pumped up about it all,
as you can imagine.

What's that, officer?
No, I didn't really get to see what they looked like.
One of 'em was wearing gloves, though.
Thought he was about to rescue me.
Picked me up, he did, and stroked me.
Then, just as before, WHACK!

This went on for about ninety minutes.
The lengths people go to get their kicks!
Demoralizing, it was. Deflating.
Didn't think I'd ever come round.
Anyway, officer, I hope you find them.
I know you won't let me down.

The Magic 18-Yard Box

I will put in the box

a high, flighted ball that hangs in the air like the moon
a drilled delivery, hit hard and low, hurtling through
    a corridor of uncertainty
a measured, side-footed pass, weighted to perfection

I will put in the box

a delicate near-post chip, fragile as glass
a bending, looping, twisting ball to baffle and
    bamboozle
a hopeful, searching far-post cross that arrives like
    a question-mark

I will find in the box

an extra yard of space in which to turn and shoot
the muddied forehead of an expectant striker
a giant, scary, hairy centre-half

The box is maths. It is geometry, algebra and
    probability.
It is shapes and lines; it is space and spots.
The box is a puzzle to be solved, a case to be cracked.
It is danger and opportunity.

I shall arrive in the box unseen
and pick its lock
like an internationally renowned jewellery thief,
who finds a way past the security cameras and red
    laser beams,
to reach the gleaming goal of which he dreams.

The Ballad of Dick, Kerr Ladies FC

Let's travel back in history –
perhaps a hundred years or more –
to when women joined the factories,
building weapons for the war.

It's in a factory, our tale begins.
It was called Dick, Kerr & Co.,
in Preston, up in Lancashire,
where the River Ribble flows.

The women cheered to hear the bell
for the day was long and hard;
each break they'd have a kickabout
in the factory yard.

Then one day, the men came up
and offered them a game.
The men played tough, roughed them up,
got beaten all the same.

And soon there sprang a masterplan
on a break from the machines:
why not do it properly
and have a women's football team?

1917. Christmas Day.
10,000 gathered in the chill.
Deepdale thrilled to watch them play.
They won the game four-nil.

How crowds flocked to watch these wonders
winning time and time again,
raising money along the way
for injured servicemen.

With silky skills and bobble hats,
they became famous newsreel stars:
Florrie Redford has scored again
with help from Lily Parr!

Then, the first international:
a two-nil win v France.
What joy to see equality
and the women's game advance!

But the FA didn't like it,
women causing such a stir.
Getting bigger crowds than men!
Who did they think they were?

Women's football must be stopped!
A solution must be found!
The answer when it came along?
To ban it from their grounds.

The Dick, Kerr Ladies carried on.
They toured the USA.
But with the ban, the progress made
slowly slipped away.

The crowds went down and interest waned,
good grounds were hard to find.
For fifty years the ban went on,
the women's game sidelined.

Fast forward to the present day
and things have changed so much.
Millions watch the women's game
and cheer on every touch.

But let's not forget that factory team
who shone and led the way.
Those women from a northern town
who showed men how to play.

Season's Greetings

There are those who wish for Winter,
while others yearn for Spring,
some who thirst for Summer's warmth
or for Autumn, that they sing.

Don't get me wrong. I like them, too.
But I love another, with good reason:
all those goalden days
from August to May,
that's called the football season.

Acrostic Town FC: Matchday Squad

Finn Gertipsave
Ivor Dodgy-Ankle
Ron Outtasteam
Serge Forward
Terry Balltackle
Earl E. Bath
Lou Scannon
Evan Lee Strike
Vince Perfect-Pass
Ed Theball
Nikolaas Minute-Winner

Simon Tenterhooks
Udo Nothing
Ben Chwarmer
Sid Elined

In Pursuit of Glory

My friend's a loyal Chelsea fan.
He has been for two weeks.
Before then, it was Liverpool
until that losing streak.

He used to follow Real Madrid,
Man City and Man U,
Barcelona, Spurs and Arsenal,
to mention but a few.

I support my local team.
They'll never be much good.
Bottom of the Football League.
I'd change them if I could.

But no, alas, it's too late now:
they've gone and stole my heart.
Perhaps the glory days will come?
A goal would be a start.

Ten Ways to Avoid Passing the Ball to Anybody

Frugal
Over here! Pass the ball!
I'm afraid you'll have to get your own ball.
They don't grow on trees, you know.

Considerate
Over here! Pass the ball!
I would absolutely love to
but first we must ask the ball
if it wants to be passed.

Mysterious
Over here! Pass the ball!
What ball be that then?
Ain't no balls been passed around these parts
since that terrible, tragic night two hundred years ago.

Exotic
Over here! Pass the ball!
Pardon, monsieur, je ne comprends pas.
Est-ce que tu parles français?

Entrepreneurial
Over here! Pass the ball!
Of course, mate. It's all yours.
For £50 an hour, that is.

Deceptive
Over here! Pass the ball!
I am afraid you are mistaken.
Why, this is a beautiful white cabbage
I have just this moment purchased
from yonder supermarket.

Mythical
Over here! Pass the ball!
I am sorry but it has been ordained
by the Gods themselves
that I am forever chained to this ball
and condemned never to pass it.

Cryptic
Over here! Pass the ball!
The codeword.
You must say the codeword.

Distracting
Over here! Pass the ball!
My word! Would you look at that! Over there!
A golden chariot being pulled across the sky
by a team of flying pigs!

Bureaucratic
Over here! Pass the ball!
Certainly. If you could just be so kind
as to fill in form C/18442 and then provide me
with two passport-sized photographs.

FIFA

Never know how much we love you
Never know how much we care
We go to put our arms around you
You're playing FIFA – it's so hard to bear

Dad's playing FIFA
Do you miss us?
FIFA though the day is bright
FIFA in the morning
FIFA all through the night

Sun comes up to meet you
Moon comes up to say hello
Mum comes up to say it's bedtime
But FIFA doesn't let you go

Dad's playing FIFA
Do you miss us?
FIFA though the day is bright
FIFA in the morning
FIFA all through the night

Everybody's got the FIFA
That is somethin' you should know
FIFA isn't such a new thing
FIFA started a long ago

Romeo loved Juliet
Juliet she felt the same
When she put her arms around him
He said, 'Julie, please just one more game'

He playeth FIFA
Dost thou miss us?
FIFA yea, ain't that the truth
FIFA on thy sofa
FIFA all the time forsooth

Francis Drake hanging out in Plymouth
Armada coming 'cross the sea
When the people tried to rouse him
He said, 'First, let me take this penalty'

He's playing FIFA
He nearly missed them
FIFA on his new console
FIFA he's obsessed
FIFA that he can't control

Now you've listened to my story
Here's the point that you must see
Ain't nothing wrong with playing FIFA
But don't neglect your family

Two Varieties of Potato

The King Edward spud
comes from royal blood.
Some say that none are greater.

But if I could
I'd pick a humbler spud:
the football common tater.

Unsung Hero

Some days you'd barely notice me
but that's just the role I play:
I close down space; I win the ball;
then pass it straight away.

Yes, up and down the pitch I go,
I run and run throughout.
I do the work of three players
but I'm rarely sung about.

That's OK, I don't expect it.
Not for me the golden boot.
Success is not the same as fame;
it can take another route.

The world is full of unsung heroes:
you may not notice but we're there,
behind the scenes, we get things done,
without fuss or loud fanfare.

It All Came Out in the Wash

My sister was a fan of Real Madrid
but I only had eyes for Man U.
'The Whites are the best!' she'd frequently shout.
I'd go 'The Reds are better than you!'

One day our shirts went into the wash.
Together. Wrong cycle, I think.
But it's brought us together as never before:
now we both chant 'Come on, you Pinks!'

The Magic Sponge™

Fractured your eyebrow?
Broken your perm?
Did a crunching tackle make you squirm?
Are you the victim of a mistimed lunge?
If so, you will need the Magic Sponge™.

The Magic Sponge™
or, to use its full name,
the ALL-PURPOSE PAIN-REMOVING INJURY-
    IMPROVING
CALM-AND-SOOTHING MAGIC SPONGE™
has been DEVELOPED in conjunction
with THE BRITISH MEDICAL WIZARDRY ASSOCIATION,
and FORMULATED on the latest laboratory research
to give INSTANT relief
from the most DISTRESSING of football injuries.

Bruised your ego?
Cracked a lip?
Received hurtful comments about your kit?
Knee begun to ooze with gunge?
Why not try the Magic Sponge™?

The ALL-PURPOSE PAIN-REMOVING INJURY-
   IMPROVING
CALM-AND-SOOTHING MAGIC SPONGE™
utilizes the latest in SPONGE TECHNOLOGY
to absorb football-based pain and other agonies.
Its SECRET MAGIC FORMULA
has been perfected through the centuries
by Himalayan monks,
schooled in the mysteries of ancient scripture
and on-pitch rehabilitation.

Are you a fully-qualified physio?
Does your job leave you dizzy-o?
Find your life has got too busy-o?
Are there injuries you can't expunge?
Then why not try the Magic Sponge™?

The ALL-PURPOSE PAIN-REMOVING INJURY-
    IMPROVING
CALM-AND-SOOTHING MAGIC SPONGE™
is CLINICALLY PROVEN
to improve recovery times,
working up to FIFTEEN SECONDS FASTER
than other less magical sponges,
and can be YOURS for as little as £174.99.

FREE BUCKET OF WATER with every purchase.

And the Award Goes to ...

Billy was a diver.

He'd keep falling to the ground,
pretend he'd been clipped,
hacked down or tripped,
when there was no one else around.

I told my Dad about him.

Cheats, he said, never prosper.
So we ignored Billy's tricks –
he won no more free kicks –
although he has since won an Oscar.

Match of the Day Theme: Official Lyrics

1. Standard Version

Da da da daaa da-da da da daa,
Da daaa da-da da daa.
Da da da daaa da-da da da daa,
Da daaa da-da da daa.
Da da da daaa da-da da da daa,
Da daaa da-da da daa.
Da da da-dada-dada-da-da
Da da da-dada-dada-da.

2. Loud Version

DA DA DA DAAA DA-DA DA DA DAA!
DA DAAA DA-DA DA DAA!
DA DA DA DAAA DA-DA DA DA DAA!
DA DAAA DA-DA DA DAA!
DA DA DA DAAA DA-DA DA DA DAA!
DA DAAA DA-DA DA DAA!
DA DA DA-DADA-DADA-DA-DA!
DA DA DA-DADA-DADA-DA!

3. Quiet Version

sh sh sh shhh sh-sh sh sh shh,
sh shhh sh-sh sh shh.
sh sh sh shhh sh-sh sh sh shh,
sh shhh sh-sh sh shh.
sh sh sh shhh sh-sh sh sh shh,
sh shhh sh-sh sh shh.
sh sh sh-shsh-shsh-sh-sh,
sh sh sh-shsh-shsh-sh.

4. Silent Version

Kit

She worked all the hours she could get,
volunteered for overtime.
Earned just enough to pay the bills
with a little put aside.

She made sacrifices where she could,
found ways to save, cut costs:
not much of a holiday that year,
made do, re-used, darned socks.

Until one day, she'd done it.
The pennies had turned to pounds.
She put on her coat, picked up her bag,
began the long walk into town.

Later on, she smiled and watched him
as the wrapping paper ripped.
The best birthday present ever:
his team's brand-new kit.

He dashed upstairs to try it on
and that night slept in it,
Dreaming of what he'd buy his mum
when football made him rich.

On Being Left Out of the England World Cup Squad

It's not sour grapes, honest.
I don't mind not being picked.
I appreciate it would have been a risk,
having not played since last Thursday lunchtime
and that horrific knee tear

to my new school trousers
(the sound of ripping polyester haunts me still).
Mum has calmed down a lot now
and I like to think she'd have supported my selection,
had she still been talking to me.

No, it was the manner of discovery.
No phone call from the manager to explain the
   decision.
Not even a text. Instead, the six o'clock news
and a man in a shirt talking about me:
It was his failure to master the language

of the post-match interview
that, in the end, led to his omission.
And he may well be right
but it still makes me feel as sick as a carrot.
I couldn't be any less under the moon.

Messi vs Ronaldo

I was on the side of Messi.
'The best player there's ever been,' I said.
'A mesmeric magician of matchday miracles.
A cunning conjuror of transcendental trickery.
A spellbinding sorcerer of sensational strikes.'

'Enough alliteration,' you said. 'Ronaldo's the best.
Such athleticism, power and presence.
Free-kicks, headers, volleys. He can do it all!
537 goals across all competitions.
How many has Messi scored?'

I declined to answer,
reminding him that as this was a poem,
should it ever get published in a book,
such statistics as that would date quickly,
and he would appear very foolish indeed.

To settle things,
we went to ask Mum who was best.
'Best? Who's *Best*?
Have you never heard of Georgie Best?
Now *there* was a genius,' she said.

Life Cycle of a Football Manager

Move to new club.
Proclaimed Saviour.

 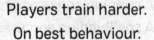

Players train harder.
On best behaviour.

Club announcement
on your sacking.

Statement from
board: get full backing.

Results improve.
Fans are pleased.

Blame injuries.
In bottom three.

Manager of the Month.
Move up the league.

Crowd gets restless.
Fall down the league.

A good cup run.
Next England boss?

Fight at training.
Best player leaves.

Expensive signing.
Unexpected loss.

A shock cup exit.
Two home defeats.

Every Day is Like a Cup Final

Mum said I should treat every day like a cup final.
Each day is special, she told me,
and we never know if it might be our last one
but what we do know
is that there will never be another one like it.
It's up to us to make the most of each and every one.

And that's what I do now.
I wake up with butterflies in my stomach
as I imagine the day ahead.
A few gentle stretches and then I head downstairs
where I make sure to eat a good breakfast
before leaving the house.

I smile at passers-by as I walk along.
Some of them even smile back.
They're probably all coming to the match later
or will settle down to watch it on TV.
No one ever asks me for my autograph,
but perhaps they're shy.

And then I arrive at the famous twin towers,
or 'school', as it's more properly called.
I used to dread it but now I look upon it
as my very own Theatre of Dreams
(and Theatre of Maths and Science and French etc.).
I imagine the cheers as I go through the gate.

I talk with my team-mates before classes begin,
doing my best to make them laugh.
Morale is critical and a joke or two
can really help to calm the pre-match nerves.
We'll need to look out for each other out there.
Then the whistle ('bell') goes and we're off!

I give it my very best.
I don't let the occasion get the better of me.
I hear the teacher over the roars of the crowd,
get my head down and put in a shift,
not shirking a tackle, coping with all the rough stuff
that might get thrown at me (e.g. equations),

always looking to go forward at every opportunity,
an eye on the goal at all times.
And the posters on the classroom walls
are flags and streamers in my team's colours,
the whiteboard is a half-time team talk,
textbooks are matchday programmes,

and there are some days
when I could just run and run and run.
I don't always win, of course,
but it doesn't stop me from feeling like a winner.
And on the days when Dad picks me up
at the end of the game

and we go to visit Mum,
and we dig up the old flowers
and he hands me the fresh ones to plant,
it feels like the flowers are the Cup,
and I'm holding it up to her,
and I'm saying, Mum, this is for you!
Just look at it! Just look at what we've done!

Back of the Net

I've been counting the holes in the back of the net.
I'm on 103 and I've not finished yet.
Who would have thought there'd be so many holes?
I count them whenever I let in a goa—

I've been counting the holes in the back of the net.
I've seen fewer holes in a Swiss cheese baguette.
The number – so far – totals 208.
Here's another attack – oh, hang on, too late.

I've counted 300 holes in the back of my net.
I'm writing it down in case I forget.
It's a full-time job. The task is immense.
The net's got more holes than my team's defen—

406. I think that's the lot.
A tapestry of holes tied together with knots.
And now, in my bed, to help me to sleep,
I've begun counting holes when I used to count sheep.

Gabriel Gómez, Number 543

I don't care for Neymar, Modrić or Messi.
Please no more Ronaldos or Dele Allis.
Till the two of us meet, my life's incomplete . . .
Gabriel Gómez, number 543.

O elusive Panamanian midfielder!
There's a gap in my album where you need to be.
Cos I'm stuck on you but you're not stuck on me . . .
Gabriel Gómez, number 543.

I've got no packets left so I guess that is that.
But hang on, what's that hiding under the cat?
I tear it open and – there! Who do I see?
It's Gabriel Gómez, number 543!

My money's all gone, unfortunately.
But it was worth every penny, I'm sure you'll agree
for Gabriel Gómez,
number 543.

End of Term Report

Maths

Good progress. Has now mastered addition
   (45 + 45 = 90 etc.).

Created some lovely triangles in midfield.

Needs to work on narrowing angles when in goal.

Physics

Really beginning to make waves.

Some great strides with his momentum and
   acceleration.

Next term, we'll be focusing on how to bend a
   free-kick.

English Language

His post-match interview skills are obviously
   coming on.

He just needs to make sure he says the word
   'obviously' enough

in general conversation, obviously.

English Literature

Lacks concentration. His defensive mix-up
with some of his team-mates at the end of last term
became a right Comedy of Errors.

Geography

Poor spatial awareness. Goes missing during games.
Looking forward next term to see his work on Cities
(once we have finished our topic of Uniteds).

History

Terrific knowledge of former FA Cup and World Cup
    winners
but needs to work more on his understanding
of late nineteenth-century Paraguayan football.

Chemistry

Generally showing good chemistry with team-mates.
Some wonderful work in the lab: the football he
    created
out of polyurethane polymers was excellent.

Biology

Seems on track with his work on diet and nutrition.
Getting hold of his essay on overstretched muscles
is proving to be quite a strain.

Modern Languages

Hopeless! He still only knows a few words and phrases:
La Liga, libero, Rabona, Ballon d'Or, vuvuzela,
Allez les Bleus!, ola Mexicana and *futebol*.

Woodwork

Hit five times in total last term.
Needs to be more careful with his shot placement.

Overall Comments

A mixed report but with some encouraging signs.
I hope to see you go forward next term
and make progress with your goals.

Dangerous Dave Damage

Dangerous Dave Damage
from Dagenham East
is a brute of man,
half-defender, half-beast,
a mis-wired fuse box,
he often sees red

and at night,
tucks his dollies
into their beds.

Dangerous Dave Damage
from Dagenham East,
Destroyer of Shin Bones,
deranged Fouler-in-Chief,
Early Bath Scrubber,
King of the Sin Bins,

wears his nan's pinny
when making
his din-dins.

Dangerous Dave Damage
from Dagenham East,
five-time winner of 'Player
I'd Like to Play Against Least',
the Scourge of Referees,
Psychopathic Leg-Scyther

is currently hiding
in his bedroom
from a spider.

The War on Cliché

How refreshing it would be,
if football managers were to take it
three games at a time,

and regard the season ahead
not as a marathon,
but a sprint.

I would love to hear about a player
who could walk his socks off
and give it 107 per cent,

demonstrate a slow turn of pace,
or find himself guilty
of a schoolboy achievement.

Some games should be five-pointers
or have nil-nil spoken all over them.
More needs to happen late doors

and home goals should count double.
I believe the time has come for formbooks
to be thrown in through windows.

Just for once, I would like to talk about
the comedy of the cup
or away fixtures that are potential apple skins.

And we should never forget
that football is a game of ninety-six minutes
(if you include time added on)

or, should it happen to go
into extra time,
a game of four halves.

Penalty Shoot-Out

one kick	**1**-0	
	1-**1**	after another
each team	**2**-1	
	2-**2**	hoping
the other	**3**-2	
	3-**3**	will miss
goalkeepers	**4**-3	
	4-**4**	guessing
diving	**5**-4	
	5-**5**	and stretching
ball avoiding	**6**-5	
	6-**6**	all fingertips
how much longer	**7**-6	
	7-**7**	until someone
slips up	**8**-7	
	8-7	. . .

this, then, for the cup . . .

Today's Results

<u>Ice Cream Premier League</u>

Aston Vanilla 0 Rotherum and Raisin 3

Strawberry Town 1 Nottingham Toffee 0

Inter Magnum 2 Chocolate Athletic 0

Mintchocchip United 1 West Bromwich Ice Lolly 2

Accrington Sorbet 1 Middlesbrrrrrrrrh 99

(with a flake on top)

The match between FC Calippo and Real Cornetto
was postponed due to a frozen popsicle.

<u>Back to Front Cup, Dnuor Tsrif</u>

Looprevil 4 Notlob 3

Lanesra 0 Snod KM 2

Nemerb Redrew 0 RPQ 0

Rafrof 3 Elav Trop 2

<u>Premier Shield Cup Trophy, Championship League Two</u>
Everton 8 Evertoff 0
Grimsby 0 Not-quite-so-Grimsby 1
Motherwell? 1 Yes-she-is-thanks 3
Sheffield Wednesday 1 See You Thursday 2
Barcelonely 0 Re United! 4
Reading 0 0 Glasses
And earlier, in today's local derby, it finished
Derby 1 Derby 1 (Derby won 5-4 on penalties).

Question Time

What happens to time
when you're winning one - nil
and there's five minutes left
but it seems to stand still?

What makes Old Father Time
start to slow down?
Why do the hands of the clock
stop going round?

Must it take an eternity
before you can win it?
Just how many seconds
can a minute fit in it?

And what happens to time
when you're *losing* two - one
and there's five minutes left
then it's suddenly gone?

Until the Final Whistle Blows

Whether top flight star or ten leagues below,
there's one thing every player knows:
the game's not over till the ref says so,
when the final whistle blows.

The books of statistics and records all show
how the seasons come and the seasons go,
the goals dry up and the body slows,
then the final whistle blows.

But why play for time and run the clock down,
waiting for that final whistle to sound?
The game's yours for the taking – you're in control –
and it only takes a second to score a goal.

Post-Book Analysis

Overall, I think he'll be happy enough with the result.
There were one or two promising touches
early on in the book
and some encouraging link-up play
between a few of the poems.

It was good to see
how the haikus settled in
with their new team-mates.

He needs to work a bit more
on his set pieces
and tighten up his metaphors
but that'll be something for him to figure out
on the training pitch,
or the drawing board,
or whatever it is that poets use to write on.

And he'll have been disappointed
to concede this last-minute poem
just when he thought
it was all over.

It is now.

About the Poet

Brian Bilston is a box-to-box poet, who can be dangerous at dead ball situations. He began his career with AFC Twitter, where he won the much-coveted 'Poem of the Season' award with a volley of verse from twenty-five yards – an achievement he celebrated with an open top bus parade and his first poetry collection, *You Took the Last Bus Home.* His good form was noticed by the selectors and Bilston was shortlisted for the Costa Prize squad for his debut novel, *Diary of a Somebody.* After a lengthy spell on the side-lines nursing a paper cut, Bilston returned to first-team action in the 20/21 season, with a new collection of poetry, *Alexa, what is there to know about love?* Off the pitch, his hobbies include watching football, listening to football, and just sitting quietly next to a football, while his favourite pre-match meal is beans on toast.